Feyesper
and the
Wicked Neighbor

Written by

Reynaldo Encina Jope

Illustrated by

Floyd Ryan Yamyamin

LifeRich Publishing is a registered trademark of The Reader's Digest Association, Inc.

LifeRich Publishing books may be ordered through booksellers or by contacting:

LifeRich Publishing
1663 Liberty Drive
Bloomington, IN 47403
www.liferichpublishing.com
1 (888) 238-8637

ISBN: 978-1-4897-1783-2 (sc)
ISBN: 978-1-4897-1782-5 (hc)
ISBN: 978-1-4897-1784-9 (e)

Print information available on the last page.

LifeRich Publishing rev. date: 06/18/2018

To Leo

Thank you all for welcoming Feyesper and his friends during their memorable debut in *Feyesper and the Rogue Kite* (2014).

Special thanks to Kaiden Juarez, a former student of mine, who introduced me to jerboas for the very first time.

Special thanks also to my most adorable three-year-old pal, Daniel Adan Lopez, who is the reason behind the name I coined: Picudanny.

A Note to Parents and Teachers

Thank you so much for your interest in Feyesper's adventure stories!

In Feyesper's first book, *Feyesper and the Rogue Kite (2014)*, we learned to use a kite to teach our kids how to keep any relationship in life healthy.

In this second adventure story, *Feyesper and the Wicked Neighbor*, we fervently hope to teach our kids empathy, tolerance and understanding.

Please don't forget to read the Autosophics pages at the end of the book. Said pages contain questions we should ask our kids, like:

> Do you wish people have a big heart for you?
> Do you wish to have a really big heart for others?
> What if we all have big hearts for each other?

These questions are intended to serve one purpose: to facilitate the germination and nurture of empathy, tolerance and understanding in our children's hearts.

Suggested Activities: Ask your kid if he/she knows of a situation that is similar to Picudanny's. This situation may come from a real-life event or from a TV show or movie for children. Feel free to use some of the questions from the Autosophics pages. Then tell your kid a Mommy's or Daddy's personal story that also mirrors Picudanny's. Use this story to usher your kid closer to a world of empathy, tolerance and understanding.

Like you, it is my hope that your kids and the children of the 21st century could live in a better, wiser world for them!

Very sincerely yours,
Reynaldo Encina Jope

Wut!

The battery indicator is extremely fidgety, so Feyesper takes his phone to his bedroom upstairs where the charger is.

"Hi, Kevin!" Feyesper greets the lone electric socket near his bed. "How are you doing today?"

"Please don't call me Kevin," the sleepy socket says. "You know that is not my real name."

"You're always home alone, Kevin," Feyesper says. "The name suits you way better. Trust me." Feyesper glances at the movie poster on the wall. The boy featured on it breaks into a knowing smile as he shakes his head.

HOME ALONe
IN THE JUNGLE

"Do you want me to help you charge your phone?" Kevin asks.

"Yes. Do you mind?"

"Not at all," Kevin says after an amplified yawn. "I can charge your phone while I take a nap. Just make sure it's off."

The pink fairy armadillo complies and sets his device down to charge. The battery indicator now looks fairly calm. Feyesper tiptoes out as Kevin's snores begin to fill his bedroom. As soon as he closes the door behind him, the doorbell rings.

"I got it, Mom!" he tells his mother as he goes downstairs. A delicious aroma of his favorite caldo de arroz, a rice soup, now permeates the living room. Mrs. Ayebeeb has been cooking in the kitchen.

Who could it be? he wonders. Feyesper opens the door but sees no one. "What is going on?" He steps out to the porch to catch whoever it was that rang the doorbell. "There's no one, Mom," Feyesper says. But shortly after he closes the door, the doorbell rings again.

Feyesper quickly opens the door and chases after whoever presses the doorbell. This time he sees the prowler right before he disappears behind a row of bougainvillea. "It's Picudanny, Mom!" he angrily reveals to his mother. "I'm sure it's him." Picudanny, a jerboa, lives right next door. His family just moved in next door a few days ago.

The doorbell rings again. It has never sounded as infuriating as it just did! Feyesper opens the door to find Picudanny standing on the porch. The jerboa flashes a very wicked smirk. As if he hadn't done enough to provoke Feyesper, Picudanny does the Harlem shake while making faces. Before the young, pink fairy armadillo can figure out what to do, the jerboa runs away, never to return.

Feyesper is now furious. He begins to plot his retaliation, but Mrs. Ayebeeb preempts him.

"Take this next door, son." Mrs. Ayebeeb instructs Feyesper to give Picudanny's family a bowl of the caldo de arroz she has just made.

"But why, Mom?" Feyesper protests angrily. "After what he has just done to us, you would do this?"

"Yes, my son." Mrs. Ayebeeb's voice is surprisingly calm. "Go, son, before it gets cold."

Feyesper does not approve of this gesture at all. In fact, he feels betrayed that his own mother seems to be indifferent to how he feels. How could she do this to him? But Feyesper is not going to disobey his mom. With so much resentment in his heart, he takes the bowl of soup and turns carefully to head out the door.

As if adding insult to injury, Mrs. Ayebeeb says, "Make sure to wear a smile, son."

His heart squelched!

"Hello, Sir Royin!" Feyesper manages to say with a smile as Picudanny's dad opens the door. He catches a glimpse of Picudanny who is hiding behind the couch.

From where he is standing he can see Picudanny's mom, Hilri. She sits on a wheelchair next to the dining table. She looks sick. In fact, she looks very, very sick! Her babushka, a head scarf, is no match to her cheerless eyes, emaciated face, and extremely pale skin. Feyesper is stunned!

Picudanny's dad graciously accepts the bowl of soup. He just got home from a long day of hard construction work, yet his face is a canvas of happiness and gratitude.

"Please tell Mrs. Ayebeeb that Hilri and I are grateful for your generosity."

"I will, Sir Royin." Before the door behind him closes, Feyesper catches a glimpse of Picudanny one more time. This time his young neighbor has revealed himself from hiding behind the couch. He doesn't seem to be wicked anymore.

Feyesper runs back home to find Kevin still asleep. He is glad his phone has been fully charged. He tells it to call his friend Oyel.

Unbeknownst to Feyesper, Mrs. Ayebeeb followed him upstairs. She is close enough to hear him speak to his phone.

"Oyel, I wonder if you would like to meet a new friend of mine."

"Of course!" Oyel, a golden snail, says. "Who?"

"Picudanny."

It seems that Mrs. Ayebeeb doesn't need to explain herself to Feyesper anymore. She walks quietly down the stairs. Each step she takes is a countdown. Her son is up for an exciting adventure of a lifetime, one that is epic—maybe beyond.

Autosophics[*]

1. Who is Picudanny?

2. What did Picudanny do that made Feyesper so upset?

3. If you were Feyesper, would you be upset also?

4. How did Mrs. Ayebeeb respond to Feyesper's anger toward Picudanny?

5. What did Mrs. Ayebeeb ask Feyesper to do?

6. Did Feyesper approve of this gesture?

7. Do you approve of Mrs. Ayebeeb's gesture?

---

[*] I coined the term Autosophics from *auto*, self, and *sophos*, wisdom.

8. Why do you think Mrs. Ayebeeb asked Feyesper to take the bowl of soup next door?

9. How did Feyesper's visit next door go?

10. Why do you think Picudanny hid behind the couch?

11. What did Feyesper see that stunned him?

12. What do you think was happening with Picudanny's mom, Hilri?

13. Why do you think Picudanny came out of hiding?

14. How did Feyesper feel about Picudanny after the visit? Was he still angry with the jerboa?

15. After the visit next door, did Feyesper now approve of his Mom's gesture?

16. Why do you think Feyesper now wants to be Picudanny's friend?

17. In your opinion, will Picudanny be a good friend to Feyesper?

18. Have you been rude like Picudanny before?

19. Have you been upset like Feyesper before?

20. Have you shown empathy for someone?

21. Should we learn to try to tolerate each other as much as we can in this world?

22. Does Mrs. Ayebeeb have a big heart for Picudanny?

23. Do your Mom and Dad have big hearts for you?

24. Do you have a big heart for Mom and Dad?

25. Who else has a big heart for you? Do they make you happy?

26. Do you wish more people have a big heart for you?

27. Do you wish to have a really big heart for others?

28. What if we don't have big hearts for each other?

29. What if we all have big hearts for each and everyone?

30. What did Mrs. Ayebeeb teach Feyesper?

31. One more time: Who is Picudanny?

Suggested Activities:

Ask your kid if he/she knows of a situation that is similar to Picudanny's. This situation may come from a real-life event or from a TV show or movie for children. Feel free to use some of the questions from the Autosophics pages. Then tell your kid a Mommy's or Daddy's personal story that also mirrors Picudanny's. Use this story to usher your kid closer to a world of empathy, tolerance and understanding.

Lightning Source UK Ltd.
Milton Keynes UK
UKHW050635020622
403879UK00005B/124